CONTENTS

The Author

Stephanie Dagg

Stephanie Dagg lives in Innishannon, County Cork.

She is a mother of two children, Benjamin and Caitlín, and has been writing stories ever since she was a child. Originally from Suffolk in England, she moved to Cork in 1992.

Mentor Press are delighted to be publishing the first three children's titles from this exciting new author: *Oh Mum!, The Witch's Dog* and *Escape the Volcano!*

Dedicated to the memory of
my mother, Eileen

1 Arriving at the Gîte

'Here we are – our home for the next two weeks!' announced Mum. 'And the weather is a whole lot better than what we left behind in Cork!'

Mrs Donoghue stopped the car outside the old, two-storey farmhouse. Tom, who was nine, and his best friend Kevin Murphy, snapped open their seatbelts and tumbled out of the car.

'Actually, Mrs D,' laughed Kevin, 'you should say that in French since we're in France now. So, what would it be? *Ici notre maison pour . . . pour . . .*'

'*Pour deux semaines*,' finished Tom triumphantly.

'Sounds right to me!' laughed Mum. 'I'll wake up your sleepy sister and then we'll go exploring. Get the key to the gîte for me please, Tom. It's in the glove compartment.'

Tom clambered back into the car and fished around for the large key. The glove compartment was crammed with sweet wrappers, maps and spare light bulbs for the car. Meanwhile Mum lifted a drowsy Anna out from the back seat. The three-year-old moaned and grumbled.

'Come on, wake up, sleepyhead!' urged Mum. 'Look, we've arrived at our holiday gîte. It's a wonderful house, look!'

Still Anna refused to wake up properly.

'Come on,' said Mum again, a bit impatiently this time. 'I can't wait to look around inside!'

'Here's the key,' called Tom at last.

'OK, open up!' said Mum.

Tom sprinted for the front door. Kevin launched himself after him. Mum stumbled along as quickly as she could with Anna in her arms.

It took a couple of turns before the lock creaked back and the heavy door swung open. Mum, Kevin and Tom hurried inside.

'All dark!' squeaked Anna.

She was right, it was very gloomy, apart from the shaft of sunlight that had followed them in.

Mum plonked Anna down. 'Of course it's dark, we need to open the shutters. Oh, but isn't it lovely and cool!'

'Yes,' agreed Kevin. 'It was getting a bit hot in the car.'

'Moaner!' teased Tom as he struggled with the big wooden shutters on the nearest window. 'Stop complaining and give me a hand!'

Mum opened three lots of shutters before the two giggling boys managed to open theirs. Gradually the kitchen filled with bright sunlight, revealing a huge room with flagstones on the floor, the biggest fireplace Tom had ever seen and beautiful old wooden furniture. The three windows along the back wall looked out over some rolling green fields. Then there was a wood, and beyond that, the Puy de Canard, a conical volcano. It was just one in a chain of dormant volcanoes that spread as far as the eye could see.

'Wow!' gasped Tom as he gazed out.

'Oh!' sighed Mum. 'What a view! And what a wonderful room this is!'

Tom stole a look at Mum. Her face shone. She was happy – really happy. Not that false sort of happy that she put on so often these days, thinking the children didn't notice. No, this was like Mum used to be before Dad died. Real smiles, real laughter, real joy.

But would she say it? Would she say it and go all sad again? Would she say: 'Dad would have loved this!' Mum was always saying that. Or 'Dad would have been so pleased with you,' when Tom had done well at school or won a swimming race or something. Or 'I wish Dad could be here.'

Tom knew Mum was just trying to keep Dad alive for them so they wouldn't forget him, especially Anna who had been so small when he died. But talking about Dad only made Mum sad – even after nearly two years.

Suddenly Mum turned her head and caught Tom's eye.

'I wonder if she knows what I'm thinking!' thought Tom, a bit guiltily.

But Mum just smiled again, even more happily.

'This is going to be a brilliant holiday,' she announced. 'Come on, let's explore the rest of the house.'

2 A Magnificent Home

It took ages to go round the whole house. As well as the kitchen, there was a bathroom with a very deep but very short bath. Kevin was horrified.

'You can't lie down in that!' he complained. Then he saw the bidet. 'What's that for, Mrs D?' When Mum explained what it was, poor Kevin looked even more horrified.

Upstairs there were two large bedrooms. Tom and Kevin chose the one with the view towards the volcano.

'I don't want to miss it erupting!' Tom joked.

Mum and Anna took the other bedroom. There were loads of cupboards and drawers, all of which had to be carefully inspected.

Back in the kitchen, the two boys found a small doorway. It wasn't locked, so Tom and Kevin decided to investigate. Stone steps led down to an enormous cellar, but the boys were rather disappointed to find it was completely bare.

'Huh, you think there'd be treasure chests or something!' moaned Kevin.

Then they all went outside to poke around the outbuildings. There was a small wooden barn.

'Perfect for the bikes!' said Mum.

Beside the barn was another small shed-like building.

'Perfect for a den!' whispered Tom to Kevin.

The shed had a small barbecue in it and lots of rackets, bats and balls. Anna brought them all out and they had a go at tennis, cricket, football and bowls.

Lastly they explored the magnificent garden. Like everything else, it was big. There were two huge apple trees, a cherry tree and a hazelnut tree, all great for climbing. Tom was pleased to see some roses and pansies, Mum's favourite flowers. He wanted everything on this holiday to be just right for Mum.

And then it was time for a small snack. They sat in the garden and ate the last few bits of food they'd brought for the journey through France. The crisps were all squashed (Kevin had sat on them!) and the chocolate snack bars had melted in the heat, but no one cared. In fact no one even noticed, they were all so thrilled with the gîte.

'We'll go into Bambert for a meal tonight,' said Mum when they'd finished eating. 'I can't face shopping today after that long drive. We'll do it tomorrow.'

'Oh,' said Tom disappointed, 'I wanted to climb some volcanoes tomorrow.'

'We might have time,' smiled Mum. 'But don't forget, we have two whole weeks. We'll climb up loads of volcanoes and go on loads of bike rides. First thing tomorrow we'll go to the tourist office and find some maps and guidebooks and things.'

'OK,' said Tom, still a bit disgruntled. Gazing up at the craggy-sided crater at the top of the Puy de Canard, he wished he could climb up it at once. He was fascinated by volcanoes. And it was for him that Mum had chosen the gîte, because it was so close to this dormant chain.

'Right, you guys!' sighed Mum, reluctantly getting up. 'Time to unpack.'

Tom and Kevin groaned loudly.

'Come on, it won't take long,' urged Mum. 'Then we'll head into town for some tea. And you can choose where we go, OK?'

'Do you think there'll be a McDonald's?' asked Tom hopefully.

'I hope not!' grinned Mum. 'I didn't come all the way to France to eat burger and chips. France is the gastronomic centre of the world, you know.'

'Isn't gastronomy something to do with stars and planets?' asked Kevin.

'No, that's astronomy silly!' chuckled Tom, throwing grass at Kevin. 'Gastronomy is . . . er . . . well, it's something else,' he finished lamely.

'Ha, you don't know either,' smirked Kevin. 'What is it, Mrs D?'

'Well, it isn't burger and chips, that's for sure,' smiled Mum. 'Gastronomy is the science of good eating.'

'But that's just what good eating is – burgers and chips!' shouted Tom, and he raced off into the house. Kevin chased after him, shouting 'Burgers and chips!' too. Anna joined in the noise. Mum covered her ears.

3 A trip to Bambert

When all the unpacking was finished they drove down to Bambert, the nearby town, in search of a proper meal. They wandered round for a good hour or so, popping into one or two shops and reading the menus outside the bistros and restaurants. Tom found one that looked really nice. It specialised in *gaufres,* which Mum explained were giant pancakes.

'Sounds yummy!' said Kevin.

'Come on, let's go in then,' said Tom. He marched up to the door to open it, but it didn't budge. He rattled it. Definitely locked.

'Hey, Tom,' hissed Mum. 'Try not to break the door down. Let's see.' She peered at the various handwritten notices on the door. 'Oh bother! This one says *Fermeture annuelle, 14–21 juillet.*'

'What does that mean?' asked Tom.

'It means it's shut all week. The owners have gone off for their holidays,' explained Mum.

'But they can't do that while we're on our holidays,' protested Kevin. 'Now we won't get any pancakey things.'

'There's always next week,' soothed Mum. 'Come on, let's try the next street.'

As they turned the corner, Mum covered her eyes and let out a cry.

'Oh no, I don't believe it!' she groaned.

The four of them were standing outside a small MacDonald's restaurant.

'Hooray,' shouted Tom, Kevin and Anna.

'Boo,' said Mum.

'Come on, come on, you promised,' laughed Tom, pulling Mum by the arm. 'You said we could choose and we choose McDonald's!'

'OK, I'm outnumbered this time,' smiled Mum. 'I surrender. But I'll get my own back. I'll get you boys into a proper French restaurant one day.'

'But Mrs D, this is a proper French restaurant,' announced Kevin. 'Well, it's French and it's a restaurant so there you are.'

'You're too clever by half, young man!' said Mum. 'Come on, let's get it over with!' And with that they all trooped in.

It was the perfect end to the day for Tom as he sat in a window seat, hungrily demolishing his burger and chips. France was fun and Mum was happy. From his seat, Tom could see the stark row of distant volcanoes standing out against the setting sun. There was only one cloud on the horizon – the prospect of shopping next day. He hated shops!

4 The Hypermarket

Normally Tom wouldn't dream of going shopping. But even he had to admit it was fun in France. First of all, it was fun trying to get the hang of francs and centimes. Then it was fun trying to convert them all into pounds and compare prices with back home.

The hypermarket they went to had to be the hugest, biggest, giantest and most enormous shop that any of them had ever seen. When they first stepped through the doors, Mum stopped in her tracks.

'Good grief!' she cried. 'This shop goes on forever!'

And so it did. Almost as far as they could see. All around them there were shelves and aisles and racks displaying goods of every description.

'Wow!' Kevin exclaimed. 'This football's half the price of the one I bought last week in Cork.'

'Really? But look, ice creams are mega dear,' complained Tom.

'Yeah, but they look much nicer than our ones!' Kevin consoled him.

'OK!' Mum laughed a little giddily. 'Let's go! Meet back here next Friday!'

The first hour flew past and they still hadn't got as far as the food hall. The boys and Anna lingered over the toys, while Mum browsed contentedly in the kitchenware section. Then she went crazy in the clothes area. Soon the trolley – big enough to fit a horse in, Kevin joked – was almost full.

Anna was thrilled to bits because there were little mini-trolleys for small children. They had tall, wavy flags attached to them so other shoppers could notice them and not run them over. Anna pushed hers happily around, popping all sorts of things in it, which Mum sneakily removed when she wasn't looking. Fortunately, Anna didn't seem to notice. They were all having a brilliant time.

Eventually they got to the food section. The first thing they came to was the fish counter. Beside it were huge tanks with all sorts of shellfish in them. The boys were fascinated, but Anna was a bit frightened. Mum was sorry to see all the poor things since they were about to be carted off to people's homes to be boiled alive.

They moved on quickly to the cheese counter. However, the smell here was so strong that Kevin went green so then they had to move even more quickly on to the meat counter. Tom spotted some horse meat and was about to tell Anna all about it when Mum intercepted him by pulling his baseball cap over his face and muttering threats in his ear.

After that, things calmed down. The children helped Mum choose the freshest fruit and vegetables, the most fattening looking pastries and puddings and all sorts of delicious French food that they had never seen before. Mum even treated herself to a bottle or two of wine.

They were exhausted by the time they got to the checkout and it took ages to unload everything. Mum looked surprised at some of the things they pulled out of the trolley.

'I don't remember buying that!' she kept muttering. 'Oh well, never mind!'

Unfortunately, she did mind the two pairs of inline skates that the boys had sneaked in.

'You've both got skates!' she pointed out.

'Yes, but these are much cooler than our boring ones,' protested Tom.

'Too bad,' said Mum unsympathetically. 'Take them back.'

She did let them keep the Action Man cycling gloves and the football though.

'Thanks, Mrs D!' grinned Kevin.

As soon as they were out of the hypermarket, they dived into the nearest café. Mum was feeling a bit weak after spending so much at one go. The children were just starving. They tucked into *frites* with mayonnaise and drank a lot of Orangina and soon everyone felt a lot better.

It was late afternoon before they got back to the gîte, loaded down with the shopping and lots of tourist information. Once the food was put away – and there nearly wasn't enough room in the fridge – Mum, Kevin and Tom sat on the lawn and waded through all the leaflets and booklets. Anna charged around trying desperately to catch grasshoppers.

'Where does she get the energy?' exclaimed Mum. 'I'm exhausted from this morning!'

Mum and the boys spent a happy hour or so planning what to see and do.

'*Please* can we go up a volcano tomorrow, Mum?' asked Tom. 'This one looks really good. Look, it's got a huge crater and you can walk all round the top. See?' He stuck a leaflet under Mum's nose.

'And how about this one!' cried Kevin. 'Look, it's been partly excavated so you can see the lava columns and the ash and whatnot!'

'Whatnot?' snorted Tom. 'That's not very scientific. You mean scoria.'

'Probably, Professor,' grinned Kevin, 'but whatnot's good enough for me. What is this scoria stuff anyway?'

'It's the lumpy pieces of molten lava that get

spat out of the volcano,' Tom told him. 'It's got lots of air bubbles inside so it's full of holes. Some bits of scoria are really tiny but other bits are really big. They're called bombs. You get different sorts of bombs depending on how gooey the lava is when it lands. If it's still squishy you get a cowpat bomb!'

Anna and Kevin giggled.

'Cor, clever you,' said Kevin, impressed. 'Where did you learn about volcanoes?'

Tom was about to say: 'Dad told me,' but he didn't want to break the magic spell that France seemed to have woven around Mum. He was afraid to mention Dad in case Mum stopped being so happy. He decided to say he'd learnt it off the Internet, which was partly true, but Mum surprised him by saying:

'Tom's Dad told him, Kevin. He was fascinated by volcanoes – he had lots of books on the subject. He loved telling Tom about them because I'm afraid I wasn't that interested,' she smiled.

Tom had stiffened while Mum was talking but when he saw her smile, he relaxed again. The spell was still holding.

5 Volcanoes at Last!

'Wow!' exclaimed Kevin, standing on the crater rim of the Puy de Canard.

'Cor!' Tom had to agree.

The two boys had run on ahead from Mum and Anna. It had taken the four of them almost two hours to get from the base of the volcano to the rim, but admittedly they hadn't been walking very fast. Anna's legs were very short and Mum could only manage to carry her for brief periods of time. So they all had to climb at Anna's pace.

Along the way they took quite a few stops to look at interesting lumps of lava or rock formations – and, of course, to have some chocolate and juice to help keep them going. But at last the boys were on top of the volcano.

Tom gazed down into the deep crater. It was huge – far larger than he'd imagined – and almost perfectly round.

'Just think, Kev,' he said, 'this is where it all happened. We're looking down on where all the lava and scoria poured out.'

'Yeah, but how come it's a crater,' said Kevin, puzzled. 'I mean, surely all the lava and stuff came out of the top.'

'Well, it was the top once,' Tom explained, remembering what Dad had told him. 'But every time a volcano erupts, it leaves a layer of scoria. The layers gradually build up around the point of emission and leave a crater.'

'Gosh, I wonder how many of those eruptions it took to build up this massive crater,' said Kevin thoughtfully. 'Mega loads, I'd have thought.'

Just then Mum panted up to join them. She too gazed in wonder into the huge crater. Anna, who had been chattering away, fell quiet.

'It's truly awesome isn't it, Mrs D?' remarked Kevin.

'It really is,' agreed Mum, smiling. 'Just let me get my breath back and then we'll climb down to the bottom of the crater, shall we? I think we can manage it OK, even though it looks a bit steep.'

She knew just how much Tom wanted to explore every inch of every volcano they saw.

'Great!' Tom whooped hugging Mum. 'Have you got your breath back yet?'

'No,' laughed Mum, 'but let's go anyway. You'll explode otherwise.'

They began to creep carefully down the steep, grass-covered slope towards the centre of the crater. Tom slithered a few times but managed to get his balance back. Kevin gave up trying to walk and took to his bottom to slide down.

'This is how to do it!' he boasted. He was certainly going much faster than the others. But he let out a few yelps as he slid over some sharp stones. Then there was a tearing noise.

'Oh no,' he howled jumping up. 'I've torn my shorts!'

'Serves you right, you show off,' teased Tom. 'I can see your pants now!'

Kevin clapped a hand over the tear in the back of his shorts and hobbled the rest of the way down. Tom made a big effort and caught up with Kevin. Even though he was his best friend, Tom still wanted to beat him to the bottom of the crater. And he did – just!

Now they were looking up the crater's sides looming towards the blue sky above them.

'How high are they?' asked Kevin.

'Hmm, I don't know really,' replied Tom. 'Maybe about twenty metres or so?'

Kevin nodded. Then he said: 'Race you to those big rocks over there!'

He hared off, and Tom chased him calling: 'They're not rocks, they're bombs!'

'OK, race you to those bombs then!' Kevin called back over his shoulder.

Kevin won easily. Tom panted up behind him.

'They're big all right, these bombs,' said Kevin, starting to clamber up one that was about twice his size.

'Be careful!' they heard Mum call. She and Anna still hadn't got to the bottom of the crater yet, but then Mum was carrying the rucksack and trying to stop Anna from falling over all the time.

Eventually they reached the bottom and went over to look at the bombs too.

'Oxygen!' she gasped. 'This time, I need a proper rest. Kevin, can you dig the goodies out of the rucksack for me. I'm too exhausted.'

So they sat by the bombs and ate their picnic.

'This,' said Kevin, 'is really cool!'

6 Alan to the Rescue

Climbing out of the huge crater was a lot harder work. Tom and Kevin took turns in pushing Anna from behind while Mum pulled her from in front.

'What a sight we must look!' laughed Mum.

Quite a lot of people were gathered at the rim of the crater. Some of them waved and Tom and Kevin waved back. But Kevin shouldn't have waved because he was on pushing duty. The minute he took his hands away from Anna, she fell down and her fingers slipped out of Mum's grasp. She began sliding back down the grassy slope on her tummy.

'Mummy!' she screamed.

Mum whirled round and plunged after Anna. But it took several seconds before Mum caught up with her and grabbed her. Even then they slithered a bit further together before coming to a halt in a heap. Anna was sobbing and Tom thought he heard Mum swearing.

'Gosh, well done, Mrs D,' called Kevin. 'And, sorry,' he added a bit lamely.

'Nitwit!' said Tom. 'We're never going to get out of this crater now and I wanted to see another volcano today. Mum will be all grumpy after this and I bet she won't let us.'

'Sorry,' muttered Kevin. 'I'll go and give your mum a hand.'

But just then a figure dashed past them. One of the spectators who was standing on the rim had come down to help. He was a middle-aged man, and obviously a sightseer in his bush-hat and baggy shorts.

'It's Superman in disguise!' grinned Kevin. But Tom groaned. 'Oh no! Now Mum'll go all huffy. She hates people thinking she can't cope, you know, on her own. I hope she won't be rude to him.'

Mum wasn't rude, but she was icily polite as the man helped her and Anna up.

'Everything OK?' he asked rather anxiously in a soft English accent. 'I'm sorry, I shouldn't have waved. All your fingers and toes still there, young lady?' He turned to Anna, took one of her hands and started to count her fingers. Anna stopped sobbing and managed a little smile.

'That's better! Now, how's your poor mother, I wonder?' he looked at Mum.

'Fine, thanks,' said Mum briskly, taking Anna's other hand quickly before the man did. 'It's kind of you to be so concerned but we're all right, really.'

Tom, listening to her tone of voice, sighed. Mum could be so snooty sometimes. After all the guy was just trying to help.

'Well, the least I can do is carry this little lass up the hill for you,' the man offered.

'No, really, we'll manage,' Mum protested.

'But I want a carry!' wailed Anna, and started sobbing again.

'Come on, just to the top,' urged the man.

Mum pursed her lips. 'Very well, if you insist.' Tom cringed at his mother's sharp response.

The man swung Anna up onto his shoulders and strode up towards the boys. Mum scrambled after him.

'Hi, I'm Alan,' said the man cheerfully, as he reached Tom and Kevin. 'I'm the idiot who waved to you from the rim.'

'And my friend Kevin's the idiot who waved back!' grinned Tom. 'Hi, I'm Tom, by the way. I love volcanoes, do you?'

'Yes, but I love caves even more. I study them. I'm a speleologist and I'm doing some research not far from here,' Alan replied.

'Wow, what are you researching?' panted Kevin, trying to keep up with Alan.

'A cave system,' explained Alan. 'There's an old troglodyte settlement in a cliff-face near here, high above the River Lune. The troglodytes were primitive people who lived in caves. Anyway, I'm sure their cave system joins up with another cave system a mile or so away. Both sets of caves share the same distinctive stratum or rock type, you see. So, I'm doing some poking around to see if I'm right.'

Alan paused to catch his breath.

'Cor, caves!' exclaimed Tom. 'Mum, did you hear that!' He turned to Mum, but she was not looking very amused.

'I'll show you if you would like,' Alan offered. 'They're not such a long way from here.'

Mum saw her chance.

'Thank you, but I think everybody's too tired today after all this climbing,' she said firmly.

'I'm not tired, Mrs D,' piped up Kevin happily. 'I could walk for miles yet! I'd love to see the caves.'

'Yes, me too,' added Tom, trying not to look at Mum. But he could feel her frowning at him!

'Me, please!' squeaked Anna.

'So, shall I show you?' Alan asked Mum.

'Looks like I'm outvoted again,' she shrugged. 'But we'll need a rest when we get to the rim.'

'Thanks, Mum,' gasped Tom, and beamed at her. Mum pulled a face. Tom knew there'd be a telling off later, but at the moment he didn't care. He just wanted to see the troglodyte caves.

7 In Search of Caves

They were soon out of the crater. In spite of his boast, Kevin's legs felt rather weary so he was grateful to flop down with the others and have some more chocolate out of the rucksack. They sat on the rim and looked away from the crater, out over the chain of volcanoes that spread far into the distance.

'What a sight!' said Tom, admiringly.

'Yeah, mega,' agreed Kevin. 'Are they all volcanoes, Tom? I mean, some of them don't have craters. Look, that one's all sort of knobbly.'

'There are different types of volcanoes, Kev,' replied Tom. 'That knobbly one is a dome, not a cone like this one we're on. You get domes when the volcano produces lava that's too sticky to flow very far.'

'Very good indeed,' said Alan, impressed. 'You know your stuff, Tom.'

'Yes, he knows all about volcanoes,' agreed Kevin. 'His dad told him.'

'Clever dad!' smiled Alan.

'Yes, he was very clever,' said Tom quietly, looking away.

Alan raised his eyebrows at Mum. 'Was?'

'My husband's dead.' Mum looked away too.

'I'm sorry,' said Alan, feeling awkward. He knew he'd intruded into private grief.

There was an uneasy silence for a few minutes but then Anna suddenly jumped up.

'Our house, our house!' she cried, pointing.

Tom leapt up. 'What? Our gîte? I can't see it.'

Kevin joined them. 'Where, Anna? Oh, yes, yes, there it is! I'd recognise it anywhere. Come and look, Mrs D!'

Mum reluctantly got up. She peered in the direction they were pointing.

'I can see a house but it's far too small to tell if it's our gîte,' she announced.

'But it is, look, there's the shed thing where we put the bikes!' Kevin persisted.

'Lots of houses have outbuildings,' said Mum firmly.

Tom looked at Mum puzzled. It so obviously was their gîte, Mum had to be blind not to recognise it. But then he saw her expression – she looked worried. Why? Of course! He groaned inwardly as the realisation dawned on him. Mum didn't want Alan to know where they were staying! She clearly wasn't happy that a stranger had taken them under his wing today. Tom knew Mum was very protective and yet Alan seemed OK. But then maybe this was a grown-up thing he couldn't understand. He must look after Mum. Dad would have wanted him to.

'No!' he blurted out. 'No way is that our gîte. We don't live anywhere near there!'

Kevin's mouth dropped open. Mum shot Tom a startled glance too.

'Kevin's brain has gone soft, Alan,' continued Tom, grinning. 'That house does look a bit like where we're staying, but it's not.'

'But . . .' Kevin began, then yelped 'Ouch!' as Tom sneakily kicked his shin. 'What . . .?'

Tom glared at Kevin. Kevin shut up at once. He didn't know what Tom was playing at but he wasn't going to ignore that warning.

'Mummy?' pleaded Anna, confused.

'Come on, honey,' smiled Mum, scooping her up. 'Shall we ask Alan to show us the caves?'

'Yes please!' came the reply. Anna instantly forgot all about the gîte, and so did the boys.

'Right, then, if you're ready, off we go!' said Alan, standing up. He didn't seem to have taken any notice of their weird behaviour. 'Shall I give Anna another donkey ride, er, Mum?' Alan asked, not quite sure what to call her.

Mum took the hint.

'I'm Jane,' she said, holding out her hand. Tom was relieved that Mum was starting to be nice at last.

'Alan, as you know!' grinned Alan, shaking Mum's hand. 'Come on, then, off we go.'

It was a pleasant walk. The descent was gentle, through shady woods. To the children's delight, they came across a dead snake. Kevin poked it with a stick.

'Ugh!' Mum pulled a face.

Then they began to climb again. Along the way Alan explained that they were walking along a lava flow.

'See how uneven it is?' he said, pointing out a lot of hollows and bumps. 'That's a particular characteristic of *cheire* – that's the French name for the lava flow. This lava came from that volcano over there.'

He turned and pointed to their left. Above them loomed a horseshoe-shaped volcano with very steep sides.

'That one's a funny shape!' remarked Kevin. 'What's the reason for that, Professor Tom?'

'I think it's because there was so much lava that it sort of washed the side of the volcano away. Is that right, Alan?' asked Tom.

'Couldn't have put it better myself,' smiled Alan.

'Tom says these volcanoes could still erupt,' said Kevin. 'Is that true?'

'Yes, technically they're just dormant or

sleeping. The last eruption in this chain was only 8,000 years ago. That's nothing in geological time. So I suppose they could erupt again.'

'Eek!' squeaked Kevin.

'But it's pretty unlikely,' added Alan. Then he turned to Mum and they began to chat. Kevin prodded Tom hard in the ribs.

'What was all that about, you know, the gîte thing. That was definitely our gîte. You must have recognised it!' he whispered accusingly.

'Yeah, I did,' admitted Tom. 'But I don't think Mum wanted Alan to know where we were staying. He is a stranger after all.'

'But he's nice!' protested Kevin.

'I know, I like him too,' agreed Tom, 'but I can tell that Mum's not really happy about him. She probably thinks he's a mad axeman or something.'

Kevin snorted with laughter at the suggestion. Tom tried hard to stay serious but soon he began giggling. The two of them sniggered for the rest of the walk. Grown-ups had the strangest ideas!

The path soon began to climb very steeply. The boys had no breath left to giggle with. Even Alan had to put Anna down and she walked the rest of the way.

'Nearly there!' he said at last. 'Just round this corner, and *voilà*! My caves!'

Mum, the boys and Anna gasped. Before

them, and rising steeply above their heads, was a craggy cliff-face, riddled with holes.

'Mega!' exclaimed Tom.

'And people lived in them!' said Mum in amazement. 'How did they get to them?'

'If you look very closely, you can see rough pathways in the rock,' said Alan. 'But it was certainly a precarious place to live.'

Mum shuddered. 'Oh, I wonder how many poor little baby troglodytes fell down this cliff!'

At the thought of the tumbling baby troglodytes, Anna got upset although she really had no idea what a troglodyte was. Mum lifted her for a comforting kiss.

'Well,' said Alan, 'it was probably less of a risk than being eaten by a bear or a puma. Living in these caves, and in a group, kept the troglodytes safer than living in conventional settlements.'

'Cool,' said Kevin, impressed. 'Were there really bears in France?'

'Oh yes,' nodded Alan. 'There were all sorts of beasts here once – woolly mammoths, wolves, sabre toothed tigers . . .'

Anna gave a squeal of alarm. Mum laughed and explained that all those animals were long since dead.

'Well, Alan,' she said. 'Thanks for bringing us. It certainly was worth the walk. But we really must start heading back now. Anna's getting tired, and I am too. You've been very kind.'

'Look, let me give you a lift somewhere,' Alan offered. 'My jeep is parked about half a mile away. You've got a long walk back otherwise.'

Mum hesitated for a moment, but a glance at the tired faces of the children decided her.

'Thanks, that would be great. Could you take us to the car park near the Puy de Canard. We can, er, get our bus from there,' she fibbed.

If Alan realised he was being hoodwinked, he didn't let on.

'No problem,' he said cheerfully. 'And maybe another day I can take you inside some of the caves. I've got torches and helmets and stuff in my jeep.'

'Could we, Mum?' asked Tom, hopefully.

'We'll see,' said Mum firmly, but Tom didn't feel quite so hopeful any more. Oh well, it had been great just seeing the caves.

'This way,' said Alan, continuing along the narrow path, in front of the caves. They all stared in fascination as they trudged past. The boys were longing to come back. They felt sad at having to leave the caves without exploring them.

But they soon brightened up when they got to Alan's jeep. It was very new, very shiny and huge. However, there wasn't much room inside. It was packed full of all sorts of equipment – ropes, torches, rucksacks, various electronic gadgets – and an axe! In fact, several!

'He really is an axeman!' whispered Kevin to Tom, giggling.

'Is all this equipment yours, Alan?' asked Mum, impressed.

'No, I'm just borrowing it from the university department for my research here. I've only got it on loan for a month so I've got to work pretty fast,' Alan explained.

'Are you a student then?' asked Kevin.

'Actually, Kevin,' smiled Alan, 'I'm a professor. I teach all the students.'

'Cool,' said Tom approvingly.

They chatted amiably for the rest of the journey. Mum asked Alan about his work and Kevin asked what all the various bits of equipment were for. But all too soon they arrived back at the car park by the Puy de Canard.

'Thanks again, Alan,' said Mum as they climbed out.

'You're welcome,' he said. 'And don't forget, I'm at the caves every day, so do please come and see me again, will you?'

'We'll try,' said Mum elusively.

'Bye boys! Bye Anna!' called Alan as he drove off.

'Bye!' they shouted back and waved till he was out of sight.

'I like Alan, don't you Mum?' quizzed Tom, hopefully.

'He seems pleasant,' said Mum grudgingly. 'But we don't really know him. And next time, please don't agree to go gallivanting off with a perfect stranger before you've asked me about it. All right?'

'Yes, Mum,' muttered Tom.

'Sorry, Mrs D. It was all my fault for waving and letting go of Anna,' mumbled Kevin.

He looked so downcast that Mum couldn't stay cross for long.

'Well, don't do it again,' she smiled, ruffling Kevin's red hair. 'I'm too tired to cook, so how about we pop down to McDonald's for tea? I'm so hungry even I fancy a burger!'

'Brill!' whooped Kevin, back to his normal bouncy self again.

'Thanks, Mum!' grinned Tom. Anna just yawned happily.

8 Something Different

They continued to explore volcanoes for the next couple of days. There was no shortage of them. One day they visited a volcano that had a lake in its crater. This type of volcano was known as a maar, or so Mum's guidebook informed them.

'Oh, Dad never told me about that kind,' complained Tom.

'He didn't know everything, love,' Mum pointed out reasonably. But Tom still felt a bit annoyed.

Another day, they went to a volcano that had been excavated. It was called the 'open air volcano' and it was amazing – well, what was left of it was. The quarrying had revealed the internal structure of the volcano and it was possible to see different layers of deposits. There was scoria from the volcano itself and also a layer of ash from the eruption of another volcano.

Tom was thrilled to see the pipe where the lava had flowed up from the magma chamber in the earth below. They could also see old lava flows interspersed with the layers of ash and other deposits. But best of all were the fossilised, carbonised trees – a remnant of a forest that had been swamped in lava by one eruption.

However, after another few days of volcanoes, even Tom was happy for a change of scene. So when Mum suggested they get up early next day and head up to Futuroscope at Poitiers, he was more than willing. Kevin wasn't particularly keen on the 'getting up early bit', but Mum assured him it would be worth it.

'So what is Futuroscope anyway?' he asked that evening over a *gaufre*. They were back in Bambert, and at last the restaurant they'd spotted on their first night was open.

'Just wait till tomorrow, Kevin,' smiled Mum. 'I promise you'll have a nice surprise.'

'I'd better have if I'm having to get up at – what time did you say?' he asked again.

'Around five o'clock should do it,' replied Mum serenely.

Kevin groaned.

'Wimp,' teased Tom. 'Are you going to finish your *gaufre*, Kev, 'cos if you're not I'll have it? I'm still starving.'

'Hands off, greedy guts. I'm just savouring it and making the taste last. I'm learning how to be a gastronaut, like Mrs D said!'

'A what?' asked Tom baffled. Mum looked puzzled too.

'Gastronaut, thicko. Remember your Mum told us about gastronomy. Well, astronauts do astronomy so gastronauts do gastronomy. Isn't that right, Mrs D?' Kevin turned to Mum for corroboration. Unfortunately, Mum was laughing too much to speak.

'Oh dear,' whispered Kevin to Tom. 'I think your Mum's had too much wine.'

'Nonsense,' retorted Tom. 'She's had too much Kevin!'

It was a good evening.

Next morning wasn't so good. They all crawled out of bed and staggered sleepily around the house, getting ready to go. Mum, who actually had had a bit too much wine after all, drank two cups of strong coffee. At last she began to wake up and she hurried the boys and Anna into the car.

It was a long drive to Poitiers. They stopped twice along the way – once for breakfast and the second time because they got lost. Poor Mum missed a turn on the autoroute, but eventually she got back on course again.

Road signs to Futuroscope started to appear. First it was 50 kilometres, then 40, then 30.

'Nearly there!' announced Mum happily.

The three children began to brighten up. They were getting bored with all the driving.

'See if you can spot Futuroscope from the road,' said Mum.

'Spot what?' grumbled Kevin. 'You haven't told us what it is yet.'

'Just keep your eyes peeled!' smiled Mum.

Three pairs of keen eyes scanned the horizon for any sign of, well, anything. Anna helpfully pointed out some horses and sheep but no one was particularly interested in them.

Just then, Tom saw a flash of metal glinting in the sun. Then another.

'I think there's a nursery garden over there,' he piped up. 'I can see the greenhouses.'

'Where?' asked Kevin.

'There,' said Tom, pointing.

Kevin looked out. 'Golly, they're really weird greenhouses, that's all I can say. One's all sort of wonky looking.'

'Yes, and look there,' said Tom excitedly. 'One looks a bit like a set of organ pipes.'

'Big round ball!' added Anna.

'Hey, is this it, Mrs D?' yelled Kevin. 'It is, isn't it!'

'Yes, well done, both of you. And here's our exit from the autoroute. We'll be there in a couple of minutes,' replied Mum.

Tom and Kevin bounced up and down on their seats with excitement. This place looked brilliant.

As they got closer, they could see more and more strange-looking buildings.

'Mega zega cool!' sighed Kevin happily.

'Wicked!' sighed Tom, equally happily.

'And you ain't seen nothing yet!' grinned Mum.

9 Futuroscope

Mum soon stopped grinning when the woman in the *guichet* told her how much it cost for all of them to get in.

'*Combien*?' queried Mum, aghast.

The woman wearily repeated what she'd said.

Mum pulled a face and handed over her visa card. 'You'd better enjoy yourselves, gang, or else!' she warned them.

'We will, don't worry!' Tom reassured her. He couldn't wait to find out what this amazing place was all about.

Although it was still relatively early in the day, the park was already thronging with people. The boys rushed through the gates, sped along the path between some buildings and then stopped dead in their tracks as the view opened up before them. Ahead of them was a sparkling lake with tall fountains and a high, arching walkway above the water. And all around were the most incredible metallic, surrealistic buildings.

'I can see why it's called Futuroscope!' gasped Kevin.

'But what's inside them, Mum?' asked Tom. 'Future furniture and stuff?'

'Oh no, much more interesting than that,' replied Mum. 'The displays are all to do with cinema and television and that sort of technology. One of these buildings houses the world's largest TV screen and another one has a 3D cinema. Anyway, let's grab a quick drink while I have a look at this guidebook to the park. We need to plan what we want to see.'

They plonked themselves down at a window table in the café. Mum went off to buy a selection of drinks and sandwiches and came back muttering about the prices again. But she brightened up after a cup of coffee and a huge sandwich stuffed with very smelly cheese. Anna and the boys sipped Orangina and argued about where to go first.

'I'd like to go to the Kinémax first. It's got a huge cinema screen. It's the wonky greenhouse building,' announced Kevin, poring over the guidebook.

'Then the Circular Cinema, definitely,' said Tom. 'That'll be mega.'

'Then the giant TV,' butted in Kevin.

'And then this Solido thing,' said Tom, jabbing his finger on the little map.

Mum chuckled as she listened to them.

'And what about you, Anna?' she asked. Anna didn't understand what the boys were on about at all. She wasn't sure what this place was all about. She looked out of the window at the park and spotted, tucked away in a corner, a playground.

'Slide please!' she decided.

'Boring,' groaned Tom, rolling his eyes upwards. 'I don't want to waste time on a slide when there's all these cool things to see.'

'Now don't moan,' said Mum. 'And remember, you will have to queue to get into all these places because they show films at certain times. Anna and I will drop you boys off at the first one you want to see and then I'll take Anna to the playground. We'll meet you when you come out. That way everyone is happy!'

The various displays were fantastic, but the boys had to do a lot of waiting around to get in. Mum and Anna went into some of them but Anna found the huge scale and loud noise frightening. However, she loved the Flying Carpet Show. This was being shown in the building that looked like a set of organ pipes. It was a cinema with a glass floor and the film was projected under the seats as well as onto the screen. The film was all about migrating butterflies. Anna really felt just like she was a butterfly too, flying along with all the others.

Mum's favourite was the Gyrotour. This was a big tower with a huge wheel-shaped lift that went up and down, giving a great view of the park. She and Anna went on it three times.

The day passed quickly and suddenly, one by one, the various displays started to close for the day. Tom and Kevin got the last two seats in the Dynamic Cinema. This was the best one of all, they decided. The film was about being on a roller coaster and the seats moved too so it felt just like the real thing. It was brilliant!

When it was over Tom and Kevin staggered outside and found Mum and Anna waiting for them in the half-light of the setting sun.

'That's it, I'm afraid,' smiled Mum. 'Everything's shut now. We'll get locked in if we don't leave soon.'

'I wouldn't mind that at all,' sighed Tom, happily. 'What a great day.'

'Yeah, super,' yawned Kevin in agreement. 'What are we going to do tomorrow, Mrs D?'

'Well, I thought perhaps we'd go and see Alan's caves,' Mum replied casually, as they trudged wearily back through the park.

The boys exchanged glances. It seemed that Mum had changed her tune since the other day! But they were delighted. They'd been bursting to go back and explore the caves properly, but hadn't dared ask Mum if they could!

So no one minded too much when they found

the souvenir shop was shut. The prospect of visiting the caves next day had put them in a good mood. However, Tom got a bit fed up when Mum couldn't remember where she'd parked the car. The Futuroscope car park was vast and Tom just couldn't face the thought of trailing around it for hours on end. But luckily Kevin soon spotted the distinctive cycle carriers on the roof so disaster was averted.

They stopped off at a motorway café for some supper soon after leaving Futuroscope. Then they began the long drive home. First Anna and then the boys fell asleep. So Mum had a lonely drive home. As they travelled further south the weather became atrocious. It lashed with rain on the windscreen and a strong wind buffeted the car. Feeling quite tired by now, Mum found herself wishing, as she all too often did these days, for some adult company – for someone to be there for her. Her thoughts turned to Alan.

10 No Croissants

'Come on, wake up!'

Tom slowly became aware of someone shaking him. Then he became keenly aware of cold raindrops splashing onto his face. He forced his eyes open. There was Mum, looking very tired and extremely wet, leaning over him through the open car door.

'Come on, love, I'm getting soaked. We're home. Here,' she said, handing Tom the huge key. 'Unlock the front door will you so I can carry Anna in. I don't want her to wake up.'

Tom undid his seatbelt and stiffly climbed out of the car. Yuk! The pelting rain soaked through his teeshirt and made him shiver. He hurried to the door of the gîte. In the light of the car's headlamps he could see a soggy yellow mess on the doorstep. Someone had obviously left a note there earlier, but the rain had destroyed it. He bent to pick it up and what was left of it turned to mush. 'Probably just a boring old circular,' he thought sleepily.

He straightened up and unlocked the door. Then he went back to the car to wake up Kevin while Mum dashed in with Anna. She took her straight upstairs to bed. When she came down she found the two boys sleepily inspecting the yellow remains of the note.

'What does it say?' asked Mum wearily.

'I don't know. I can't read any of the writing properly. It's ruined,' said Tom yawning.

'Never mind, it's bedtime for you boys. Throw that stuff in the bin and up you go. Let's hope the weather's better in the morning, hey?'

Tom and Kevin shuffled off and Mum went back out into the rain to lock the car. Then, aching with exhaustion, she did the rounds of the house, closing shutters and locking doors. Too tired to undress or wash, she threw herself on the bed next to Anna's and was asleep within seconds.

Mum woke next morning to a shaft of sunlight across her face.

'That's funny,' she thought sleepily. 'I was sure I closed the shutters last night.'

Mum turned her head towards the window and gave a shriek. Anna was leaning dangerously far out of the window, pushing the shutters open. Mum was on her feet in a split second and firmly pulled Anna away from the window.

'Anna, you must never, ever do that again,' she scolded. Anna's lip trembled. 'Come on,' said Mum, hoping to prevent the impending tears.

'I bet those boys are still asleep. Let's you and me go into the village and get some lovely fresh croissants, shall we? We'll take the bike since it's so sunny!'

Anna cheered up at once. Mum peered into the boys' bedroom and smiled to see them sprawled all over their beds, snoring peacefully. Scribbling a quick note to tell them where she and Anna had gone, she propped it up on the kitchen table. 'But they'll probably still be asleep when we get back,' she winked at Anna.

They put on their cycle helmets and Mum fetched her bike from the barn, propped it up against the car and lifted Anna into the child seat.

'Oof!' she gasped. 'I won't be able to do this for much longer, young lady! You're getting far too big.' Mum strapped Anna in and they set off.

It was a beautiful sunny, still morning – a complete contrast to the night before. The heavy rains had freshened everything up and the French countryside looked greener and more alive than before. Mum hummed happily as she cycled.

It was about three kilometres into the village along a narrow winding lane. The few farmhouses they passed were still shuttered up which Mum thought was a bit unusual since it was after seven o'clock. And the other slightly odd thing was that it was so quiet. Silent, in fact. No birdsong at all.

'Strange,' thought Mum to herself. 'Maybe yesterday's storm has upset all the wildlife.'

But Mum was enjoying the ride too much to worry about the silence for long. Anna called out the names of different things as she gazed around at the rolling hills and looming volcanoes. Then she remembered something.

'See 'lan today?' she asked.

'Yes, we'll see Alan today,' Mum smiled. Then she realised she was looking forward to seeing the Englishman again.

A few more minutes' pedalling brought them to the edge of the village. First they passed the cemetery, then the church, and beyond it the road swung round a sharp bend into the village square. On three sides there were quaint shuttered houses, and on the fourth side there was a boulangerie, a boucherie and a café tabac.

'Oh!' exclaimed Mum in disappointment, as they drew up outside the boulangerie. 'It's shut!'

And it wasn't about to open either. There was no delicious smell of baking bread and croissants. The butcher's shop and the café tabac were both closed too.

'How strange,' thought Mum.

Then her tummy gave a little rumble in complaint.

'What day is it, Anna?' asked Mum.

'Saturday?' suggested Anna, helpfully.

'Hmm. Let's see,' Mum realised she'd lost all track of time since they'd arrived in France. 'We left Cork on Thursday and got to the gîte on Friday, then we went shopping on the Saturday, volcanoes for the first time on Sunday, three more days of volcanoes, one day of Futuroscope – so that means it's Friday again. Now that's really odd because it's meant to be market day on Friday.'

But the village square was deserted.

Mum lifted Anna off the bike. 'Come on, we might as well stretch our legs now we're here. Anyway, if we wander down a side street or two we might find a shop that's open.'

Anna was happy to go anywhere, so long as she was with Mum.

'You know, Anna,' said Mum, 'I wonder if it's a national holiday today. That would explain why everyone is still in bed and there are no market stalls or shops.'

'Holiday,' agreed Anna.

'Yes, that must be it,' Mum decided. But she wasn't totally convinced.

They walked around the square, glancing down the narrow side streets that led off it, but there was no sign of activity in any of the shops or cafés. In fact, there was no sign of anyone at all. It was as if they were the only two people there.

The silence and emptiness was eerie and Mum felt a shiver go down her spine.

'Come on,' she said briskly to Anna. 'Let's get back to the boys. We'll just have to eat cereal for breakfast today.'

They headed back towards the bike. Suddenly something caught Mum's eye. It was a huge, muddy puddle in one of the narrow lanes, about fifty metres away. It spread right across the road.

'Hmm, I never noticed that before,' thought Mum. Then she blinked and looked again. The puddle was moving towards them – and quickly!

'What on earth . . .?' she exclaimed. Then she froze. She could now see that it wasn't a puddle at all. It was a dark mass of rats and it was heading straight for her and Anna.

'Oh no!' she screamed. She grabbed Anna and started to run towards a house with a doorstep outside it. But it was too far away. Within seconds the rats had caught up with them. Mum could only stand still, sobbing in horror as the animals scampered around her, some of them running over her sandalled feet. Anna clung to Mum with all her strength, burying her head in fright.

It seemed to go on for ages, this stampede of rats. But it was probably only seconds. At last the rats were gone up the lane, heading across the square and out of the village. Mum continued to stand sobbing, and now Anna joined in. They hugged each other tightly.

Mum managed to pull herself together enough to start walking towards the bike again. She was trembling all over and she felt like screaming but that would only frighten Anna. Something was horribly wrong – but she didn't know what or why. All she knew was that she had to return to the boys as soon as possible. She'd quickly pack some clothes, she decided, and they'd head off somewhere – anywhere – for a few days until life got back to normal. Yes, that's what she'd do.

Mum felt better for having a plan. She strapped Anna in her child seat and was about to climb on the bike herself when the air was split by an ear-shattering explosion. The noise echoed off the houses in the village square and shook the glass behind the shutters. The whole village rattled and rumbled.

'Bad noise, Mummy.'

It was too much for Anna. Her face screwed up and she began to cry hysterically, holding her arms out to Mum. Mum wanted to comfort her but for now her top priority was getting them both back to the gîte.

'Hang in there, Anna,' she called above the thunderous echoes and leapt onto the bike and began to pedal furiously in the direction of the gîte. But seconds later she had to pull up again as stones began to rain down on them. Mum turned and held her arms up to try and shield Anna and herself from the falling debris.

'Where are these rocks coming from?' she wondered. Then another explosion made her turn her head in the direction of the Puy de Canard. What she saw made her heart stop still with horror. The volcano was erupting! A cloud of smoke and ash was rising from its crater, and through the cloud spurts of lava were shooting high into the sky. The lava was falling as scoria and bombs – some of them on her and Anna.

'We've got to get home, Anna!' shouted Mum, starting to cycle again. 'Lean forward against me, love, and tuck your hands under your body. You're safe with Mummy.'

Mum hoped Anna would believe her although she didn't think she believed herself.

11 Erupting Volcano

Meanwhile, back at the gîte, the explosion had woken Tom and Kevin. They lay yawning and stretching on their beds.

'Wow, did you hear that thunder?' asked Kevin, sitting up. 'It sounded jolly close.'

'Yeah, it nearly shook me out of bed!' laughed Tom. 'Another wet day by the sound of it.'

The boys listened to the hammering noises on the roof and against the windows.

'Hey, that sounds like hail, and big hailstones at that,' observed Tom. 'Let's have a look.'

He padded over to the window, pulled it open and then undid the shutters and pushed them out. The sight that met him turned his face pale. His volcano had come alive! Like Mum, he saw the huge grey cloud of smoke and ash hanging over it, lit up occasionally by flashes of lightning. Spurts of red lava were shooting high into the air. And it wasn't hailstones that were falling on the house, but ash and larger volcanic debris. As Tom watched in shock, a much larger bomb of still-molten lava landed in the garden outside.

'Oh . . .!' Words failed him. To think he'd joked about seeing the volcano erupt.

'What's up, Tom?' asked Kevin anxiously, catching sight of Tom's white face. He trotted over to join his friend. 'And what's that stink-bomb smell. You haven't . . .'

Then he saw what Tom was staring at.

'Jeepers!' he gasped. 'The volcano's erupting!'

The two of them stared in horror. Then Tom came to his senses.

'Quick, let's get Mum. We've got to get out of here. We're way too close to the volcano.' He sprinted to Mum's room but it was empty.

'She must be in the kitchen,' he called as he dived downstairs. Meanwhile, Kevin was hurriedly pulling on some clothes.

But the kitchen was empty. 'Where on earth is Mum?' wondered Tom. Then he saw the note.

'*Hi, sleepyheads!*' it read. '*We've gone to get croissants for breakfast. Back soon. Love, Mum.*'

'Kev!' screamed Tom. 'Mum's not here. What are we going to do?'

Kevin thundered down the stairs. Tom showed him the note. He was trying desperately not to cry, but waves of panic were surging through him. What were they to do?

'OK, OK, let's think,' gabbled Kevin, as shaken as Tom. 'Maybe Mrs D will be back in a minute. I'm sure when she sees the eruption she'll come back for us.'

'Yes, but the village is quite a way off,' Tom blurted. 'What if she can't get back? What if the road's blocked by bombs and ash? What if . . .?' He was about to say, what if Mum's been hit by a bomb but that possibility was more than he could bear.

'OK, then, so we stay here,' Kevin went on. 'The cellar will be safe, won't it? I mean, people shelter in cellars from tornadoes and hurricanes and stuff. Well, they do in films anyway. Crumbs! What was that?'

A huge crashing noise made them jump. They ran to the kitchen window. The roof of the little building they'd used as their den now had a huge burning hole in it.

'Another bomb!' gasped Tom. 'Yes, we'd better go down to the cellar, I suppose.'

They hurried down the stone steps, but moments later they were back in the kitchen, collecting food and water to take down with them.

'We'd better get some blankets too. We may have to stay there for days,' said Kevin.

'Wait a minute, if the house collapses, then we could be there for weeks,' said Tom, falteringly. 'I remember reading somewhere that the weight of ash often makes houses fall down.'

The two boys fell silent. The prospect of being sealed into the cellar for weeks was not appealing.

'And what if no one ever found us!' gasped Kevin. 'We'd starve to death.'

'Well, we'd probably suffocate first,' Tom pointed out.

'Oh great, I feel much better now!' snapped Kevin.

'But anyway, if there's a lava flow, it would swamp the house and the cellar and . . .' Tom trailed off.

'And we'd be cooked!' finished Kevin, grimly. 'That's it, there's no way I'm going back down into that cellar.'

'You're right,' agreed Tom. 'The cellar is a dumb idea. Come on, we've got to get out of here and get to higher ground so we can escape the lava flow. We need to find some sort of strong shelter too. Maybe the church in the village?'

'That's no higher than here,' Kevin reminded him. 'Wait a minute! I've got it! I've got it!' Kevin was thrilled at being the one to get the good idea for a change.

'What? Tell me!' shouted Tom.

'The caves of course. Alan's caves! They're high up, and they'll shelter us. It won't take too long to get there either.'

'Brilliant!' smiled Tom. 'Kev, you're a genius.'

They put on their cycle helmets and jackets to protect themselves from scoria and bombs. Then grabbing a few chocolate bars they dashed outside to the small barn for their bikes. The ash and debris was raining down harder than ever. Another loud rumble came from the volcano.

The boys paused inside the barn door. They looked at each other for a moment and then grabbed their bikes.

'Let's get the heck out of here!' said Tom.

'Do you really think we'll make it?' asked Kevin.

'I honestly don't know, Kev, but what else can we do?' replied Tom. 'I wonder if should we take the car?'

'What? Us?' gasped Kevin. 'We can't drive. Well, I can't anyway.'

'No, I can't either. Stupid idea,' said Tom shaking his head. 'I just thought we'd be quicker and safer in it.'

'No, it wasn't stupid, Tom,' Kevin comforted his friend. 'It would be a lot quicker. But I reckon we should stick to the bikes. Come on, let's go.'

They wheeled the bikes out of the barn, wincing as more pieces of scoria hit them.

'Hang on, I haven't left a note for Mum!' yelled Tom. 'We must tell her where we've gone. She's bound to come back here for us.'

'Good idea, but hurry!' urged Kevin. 'Look, there's loads of lava pouring out of the volcano!'

He was right. The burning hot lava was now starting to flow, slowly but surely, down the sides of the Puy de Canard.

'Oh no! I haven't got a pen,' cried Tom, fumbling in his pockets. There wasn't time to go back into the house and start hunting. What could he do?

'I know! I'll scratch a message on the bonnet of the car!'

'What?' Kevin was shocked. 'Your Mum'll kill you!'

'This is an emergency, Kev. And anyway, if we don't get a move on, we'll really be killed!' Tom grabbed a stone and scratched two words in huge, scruffy letters. '*ALAN'S CAVES*' he wrote.

'Will she see it?' wondered Kevin.

'Of course!' Tom managed a grin. 'Mum can see the tiniest scratch on this car from a mile off!'

'True,' agreed Kevin. 'Now please, Tom, can we go?'

12 Caught in a Stampede

The two boys set off on their bikes. The falling debris was getting worse by the minute. Every now and again, they had to swerve to avoid bombs that had fallen on the road. The ash in the air was making it hard to breathe, but they kept on pedalling.

Suddenly they became aware of a tremendous rumbling noise behind them.

'Must be more lava erupting!' called Kevin.

But the noise seemed to be getting even louder and closer to them. Tom snatched a glance over his shoulder.

'Crikey, Kev,' he shouted. 'It's a herd of cows. Quick, get over by the fence or they'll squash us.'

They swerved their bikes crazily to the side of the road and huddled close together. Seconds later the terrified cows galloped by, their eyes wide with fear. There must have been sixty or more of them. The noise of thundering hooves and constant lowing was deafening.

'Poor things!' said Kevin as they passed by. 'They can't have a clue what's happening.'

'I have to say I feel a lot sorrier for us,' panted Tom. 'Come on, let's go!'

'Now we have to avoid cow-pat volcanic bombs and *real* cow-pats too!' joked Kevin.

Tom groaned appreciatively at the joke.

But round the next corner there was a shock in store. The road stretched straight ahead of them and they could see the stampeding herd streaming away. In front of the herd, and coming towards them, was a cyclist. Tom squinted through the ash-filled air.

'Kev, it's Mum and Anna!' he called in relief. But then he remembered the cows. 'Oh no, the cows will knock them down. They'll be trampled!'

'Mrs D, watch out!' yelled Kevin, uselessly.

'Mum!' shouted Tom.

With her head down to protect her face from scoria, Mum was cycling as fast as she could. Suddenly she became aware of the thundering hooves of the cows. She looked up and was met with a sea of scared bovine faces. There was no time to get out of the way. All she could do was stop and scream and wave at the cows to make them go round the bike.

The confused animals plunged in all directions. Most of them careered to the sides but a couple of them didn't, and Tom and Kevin watched helplessly as they saw Mum and Anna disappear from sight.

'Mum! Anna!' screamed Tom, tears streaming down his face. He started to pedal madly down the road towards them.

He found Mum in a heap on the ground, blood gushing from her nose and a huge gash on her face. As she fell, Mum had managed to twist and lie over Anna to protect her from the cows. Anna was sobbing, but Mum was quiet.

'She's dead! She's dead!' shrieked Tom.

'No, she's alive,' Kevin reassured him, feeling for her pulse. 'She's just knocked out. Help me sit her up so we can get Anna out from underneath.'

They heaved Mum into a sitting position, and as they did so she groaned and opened her eyes. For a moment, she looked at the boys blankly. Then her face seemed to clear.

'Tom! Kevin!' she croaked. 'But . . . Anna! The cows! Is she OK?'

'She's right here,' said Kevin, who was helping Anna up, having unstrapped her from her seat. 'And she's fine, aren't you, precious?'

He lifted Anna up and she clung to his neck.

'Thank heavens!' sighed Mum. 'But . . . ouch! I think those wretched animals had a quick game of football with my poor head as they went by. Oh!' she gasped suddenly as she tried to stand up. 'And with my ribs!'

'Mum, can you keep cycling?' asked Tom,

urgently. We need to get to Alan's caves if we're going to be safe.'

'I'll try!' said Mum.

She got up very slowly and shakily and wiped the blood off her face.

'I must look a sight!' she added wryly.

'Beautiful as ever, Mrs D!' replied Kevin, as cheerfully as he could. But the truth was Mum looked awful. Kevin caught Tom's eye. Would Mum be able to make it to the caves?

Tom bent down to pick up her bike. But the front wheel was a tangled mass of broken spokes. No one had noticed before because they'd been so worried about whether or not anyone was hurt.

'Oh no!' cried Mum. 'Look at the bike. It's useless!'

'And look at the lava,' shouted Kevin. 'It's coming this way!'

It was true. The lava seemed to be flowing faster now, sweeping steadily towards them.

'We could go back and get the car, but there's no time,' cried Mum, standing up. 'Oh gosh, my head!' Mum reeled forward and fell to her knees. Anna screamed.

'Mum! What will we do!' yelled Tom. But Mum didn't seem to hear. Her face was screwed up in an expression of agony.

Tom closed his eyes for a moment. He had to

be strong. It was up to him now to get everyone to safety. Mum was hurt, and Kevin and Anna were scared. Well, so was he! But they were relying on him to look after them. He mustn't cry or panic.

'Dad, help me!' pleaded Tom silently.

Just then Mum wobbled to her feet again.

'Right, Tom,' she said firmly. 'I want you to take Anna on your crossbar and go with Kevin as fast as you can to the caves. You know the way, don't you?'

Tom nodded. 'Yes, but what about you?'

'I'll run behind you both just as fast as I can,' said Mum. 'But don't wait for me. Don't stop. Just keep going. OK?'

Tom nodded again. But his eyes were full of tears. He couldn't just abandon Mum. She was hurt. She needed his help.

But Mum could read his thoughts because she added: 'That's an order, Tom. You get yourselves to safety. I'll catch you up.'

Mum pulled her cardigan off and quickly wrapped it around Tom's crossbar, then she lifted Anna onto this makeshift seat so she was facing towards Tom.

'Hang onto Tom and don't let go, Anna angel,' she tried to smile. 'Put your legs up around his waist so he can pedal. That's right. How does that feel, Tom?'

'OK,' said Tom, trying not to worry about Mum too much. She looked awfully pale.

Raising a bloody hand, Mum stroked Tom's cheek. 'Now go, and don't stop for anything till you get to the caves. GO!'

Tom set off, wobbling all over the road until he got used to Anna's weight on the bike. Then he got into his stride. Kevin cycled silently beside him. Tom desperately wanted to look back at Mum, but he knew if he tried to turn his head around he'd fall off the bike. His job now was to look after Anna and get her to safety.

Mum limped after them, wincing with every step, her whole body aching. Her head hurt so much she could hardly bear the pain. But she had to see the children to safety, if it was the last thing she ever did.

13 In Search of Shelter

On and on the boys pedalled, for all they were worth. They whizzed through the village, and then they left the road and turned onto a narrow track. The track began to climb steeply. Tom's throat ached as he gasped for each breath. He forced his legs to keep going. Kevin kept pace with him. They hardly noticed the scoria hitting them any more. They were focussed only on getting to the caves.

'Can you see Mum?' panted Tom.

Kevin glanced behind him. There was no one there.

'Yes, she's not far behind,' lied Kevin. 'She's doing great.'

'Thank heavens,' gasped Tom. 'Oh, it's getting steep now! Hang on tight, Anna.'

They struggled on for another half-mile but then Tom suddenly ran out of energy. His legs went weak. Anna seemed to weigh a hundred tons. 'This is hopeless,' he thought. 'We'll never escape the lava.'

Tom's head drooped with exhaustion. He was about to fall from his bike when he was sure he heard a voice. It sounded just like – Dad!

'*Come on, Tom. You can do it. You can!*'

'Dad?' said Tom out loud, looking up.

'What did you say?' panted Kevin beside him.

But Tom didn't hear. He suddenly felt someone give his bike a mighty push, just like Dad used to do when he was a boy and was getting tired when they were out cycling together. His legs began to fly round on the pedals again and he felt a new burst of energy. He could do it and he would do it. He'd get them to the caves.

'Thanks Dad!' he whispered.

'Hey, wait for me!' protested Kevin as his friend surged ahead. 'I'm meant to be setting the pace, remember.'

Making a big effort, Kevin caught up with Tom and the two boys pedalled furiously further up the track. Not far to the caves now.

'Mind the bend!' shouted Kevin back to Tom, as he hurtled round a sharp corner. Then 'Yikes!' he cried as he saw someone cycling towards him at top speed. Both cyclists braked at once and Kevin swerved to avoid a collision but lost his balance and fell. Tom heard the noise in front of him. Then he came zooming round the corner.

'Kev!' he shouted as he saw his friend on the ground. Then 'Alan!' as he recognised the person bending to help Kevin up. Tom wobbled to a halt.

'Boys! Anna!' cried Alan. 'Thank heavens you're safe. I was coming to look for you!'

Kevin stood up. 'But how did you know where we'd be?' he asked.

'Well, when I couldn't find you guys at any of the emergency shelters, I was worried. So I drove out this way to look for you. Unfortunately, a very large bomb finished off my jeep – and nearly finished me off too!' Alan pulled a face. 'I ran for a while and then I came across this bike so I started cycling.'

'Emergency shelters? What do you mean? How did you know where to start looking for us?' gabbled Tom, as Alan lifted Anna off the crossbar.

'Well, remember your *Now you see it, now you don't* routine about your gîte when we were up on the Puy the other day?' Alan smiled. 'Well, I had an idea what was going on. So I took a chance today and came out here to find you. But where's your Mum? Where's Jane?' he asked hurriedly.

'She's just behind us,' said Tom. 'She was hurt when a herd of cows stampeded. Her bike was wrecked so she made me take Anna and go on ahead.'

'Just behind? Thank goodness, I'll go back and get her and then I'll take you all to a safe place.' Alan bent down to pick up his bike but Kevin grabbed his arm.

71

'Alan, the truth is we don't know where Mrs D is!' he confessed. 'I told Tom I could see her when I looked behind, but I couldn't really. She was badly hurt, Alan. She's probably miles behind.'

'Kevin, you liar, you rotten, rotten liar,' shouted Tom. 'You said she was OK! I've got to go and get her!' Tom turned to start cycling back down the track.

'No, you stay here,' snapped Alan. 'You'll do as your Mum told you and look after your little sister. I'll go back and help your Mum, but first I'll get you three into a cave where you'll be safe. Come on, we can run from here.'

Alan lifted Anna onto his shoulders and he and the boys trotted up the track a little further. Then he led them off the track and up a smaller path.

'I'm going to take you to the other set of caves I was telling you about,' he explained. 'They're on this side of the hill so they are closer than the troglodyte caves.'

It wasn't long before they reached one of the cave entrances.

'Here we are!' said Alan, putting Anna down. 'You will be safe from any lava coming up the hill, and safe from any lava coming down!'

Swinging his bulging rucksack off his back, he pulled out some torches and a rope.

'I'm off to look for your mum now,' he told

them. 'While I'm gone, I want you to tie yourselves together with this rope – with about ten metres between you.'

'Why?' asked Tom. 'Aren't we safe here?'

'Hopefully yes,' said Alan. 'But just in case another volcano erupts or something else happens I want you to be ready to go through this cave.'

'Through the cave!' said the boys in unison.

'Yes. Now, listen carefully. Do you see this stratum of rock here?' Alan asked, pointing to a distinctive orange-yellow layer in the dark red of the rock.'

'Yes,' answered the boys, giving him their full attention.

'This orange-coloured stratum occurs in the troglodyte cave system too,' said Alan. 'If my research is right, the two sets of caves link up. By following this cave you should come out in one of the troglodyte caves on the other side of the hill.'

'Why can't we just walk round the outside of the hill on the path?' asked Kevin, who didn't like the idea of disappearing into a cave.

'No, the path we were on dips down from here so any lava will flow down it – and quickly. The best thing to do is to go through the cave. It'll work, trust me!' Alan smiled. 'Anyway, I'll be back with your Mum in no time, so you probably won't need to go anywhere. See you soon.'

He waved cheerfully and disappeared.

The children were too tired and anxious to say anything. They huddled together, gazing down the empty path. Tom's mind was racing. What if Alan couldn't find Mum? What if Mum had taken a wrong turn? She might well have done so in her state. What if Mum was hit by a bomb or the lava caught up with her?

'I shouldn't have left her!' Tom cried out, and this time he couldn't stop the tears. Kevin put his arms round his friend and let him sob helplessly on his shoulder. Little Anna just watched in bewilderment.

It was a long, long wait. Tom soon calmed down and he and Kevin took it in turns to walk a little way down the path to look for signs of Mum and Alan. Nothing. Always nothing. The only thing they could see was the lava as it burned its way closer towards them.

14 A Minor Earthquake

Alan had been frantic when he left the children. He guessed that Jane must have been pretty badly hurt to send the children on ahead of her, especially to entrust little Anna to her not very much bigger brother and his friend.

'Please let me find her!' he prayed to himself.

He'd been impressed by the small, pretty, determined woman the first time they'd met. OK, she'd been unfriendly to start with, but once Alan had learned that she was a widow, he could see why she was so protective. And after all he was a stranger. But he didn't want to stay a stranger for long. He wanted to get to know Jane a lot, lot better. 'Please let me have the chance!' he pleaded.

He reached the track and climbed on his bike. Then he went hurtling at a crazy speed towards the approaching lava. He reached the end of the track and scanned the road ahead. Nothing, nothing at all. Just falling ash and debris. He swerved quickly to avoid a huge bomb embedded in the road. And then he saw a movement. He pedalled harder. Yes, he could just make out a small figure stumbling along. It had to be her!

'Jane!' he roared. 'Jane!'

In the distance, Jane stopped and lifted a weary arm. She waved once and then fell to the ground. Alan tore onwards and screeched to a halt beside her.

'Jane! Thank heavens I've found you!' he cried, jumping off the bike.

'Hi!' gasped Mum. She could hardly speak with tiredness and pain. 'The children . . .?'

'It's OK, they're safe,' said Alan with a smile. 'They're waiting for you in one of the caves. Your son is quite a kid. Takes after his mum, I'd say!'

Jane managed a tiny smile.

'Anyway, you'll see him for yourself in a short while,' said Alan. He helped Jane up onto his bike. 'I couldn't get a taxi so this is the best I can do!' he grinned.

Jane didn't even try to protest as he started to wheel her along on his bike. She knew she couldn't walk another step. Every part of her body hurt too much.

Alan went as fast as he could. He could feel the heat from the advancing lava on his back and his legs. There were loud crackling sounds as the lava slid destructively towards them. There wasn't a second to lose. They must get back up the track to higher ground, and fast!

Back at the cave entrance, the boys and Anna waited nervously. They managed to tie themselves together with elaborate-looking knots. As they sat huddled together they could see the sea of hot lava approaching, but no sign of Mum or Alan.

'Come on, come on,' said Tom, biting his lips. Oh, would they ever come back! Peering out at the dark clouds of smoke and ash, he felt sick with worry.

'Is there any food in Alan's bag?' asked Kevin suddenly. 'I'm starving!'

Tom was about to snap at his friend that this was hardly the time for him to be worrying about his stomach, when his own stomach rumbled!

'Good idea, Kev! I'll have a look.' But as he stood up, he began to wobble. 'Wow, I must be hungrier than I realised,' he thought. But no, it wasn't him that was wobbling, but the ground!

'It's an earthquake!' he yelled.

'Isn't an eruption enough for one day?' asked Kevin, crouching down.

'Well, they usually go together!' shouted Tom, over the sound of crashing rocks. He grabbed Anna and clung on to her as the earth shook and groaned.

Then there was the grating of sliding gravel and the sound of falling rocks. The two boys glanced at the cave entrance and watched in horror as the opening slowly became blocked up. Suddenly everything went black in the cave.

'All dark!' cried Anna.

'It's OK, Sis,' said Tom. He fumbled for his torch for a few seconds. It had rolled away from him during the earth tremor, but his fingers soon touched its cold metal case. He flicked the torch on and shone the strong bright beam at the entrance. It was filled with a pile of boulders and some of the loose gravel was still sliding down. At last the ground stopped shaking.

'What next?' Kevin whimpered, still crouched down.

'We go through the cave like Alan told us, that's what's next,' announced Tom decisively. 'We certainly can't get out here. And Alan and Mum won't be able to unblock it,' he said. Tom shut his mind to the possibility that anything might have happened to the adults during the earthquake. 'So, we'd best get going. Come on Anna.' He took his frightened sister's hand. 'Kev, can you manage the rucksack? We may need it later.'

Kevin nodded. He was glad to be told what to do. He took a torch out of the rucksack for himself and followed as his friend hesitantly set off into the depths of the mountain.

15 A Maze of Tunnels

Alan and Mum had been lucky when the earthquake struck. They had just passed a small wood and were out in the open when the ground began to shake. They heard some trees crashing down behind them. Mum slid off the bike and crouched down next to Alan until it was all over.

'This is quite an eventful day!' observed Alan wryly as they set off again along the track.

'Don't worry, Jane, the kids will be fine in the cave. We'll be there in just a few minutes. At least we're high enough now to be safe from the lava.'

It was true. They could see the lava far below them now. The falling debris and ash seemed to be getting less too. 'But maybe the earthquake would set everything off again,' thought Alan to himself. It was a distinct possibility.

They abandoned the bike and started to climb up the narrow path as fast as they could. Soon they were scrambling towards the cave where Alan had left Tom, Kevin and Anna. They turned the last corner, but the cave entrance wasn't there – only a pile of rocks and stones.

'Which cave were the children in, Alan?'

asked Mum nervously as she took in the scene. She could see what had happened. 'Please tell me it wasn't this one.'

'It was, I'm afraid,' confessed Alan.

Mum gasped in horror.

'But it's OK,' Alan quickly reassured her.

'I left them with torches and a rope and told them how to get through the cave to the troglodyte caves on the other side of the hill.'

'But they're only children!' cried Mum. 'And do those caves really join up? Have you been right through them yourself?'

'Well, no,' replied Alan weakly, 'but I know they connect. All my research points to that. I was going to plot the course tomorrow.' Alan's voice faded. Suddenly it all sounded so unconvincing.

Mum bowed her head, trying not to visualise the three children lost in a tangle of underground passages or being buried by a rock fall. Had Alan sent them to their deaths? She looked up at Alan's stricken face. No, of course he hadn't. He had already saved their lives by getting them to the caves safely. And he'd prepared them for any emergency. She knew he had done all he could for them all, and more. She trusted him. The children would get through. She squeezed Alan's hand.

'Come on, then, let's be waiting for them when they come out the other side,' said Mum.

Meanwhile, Tom, Kevin and Anna were actually starting to enjoy their adventure. It was pretty spooky in the cave to start with, especially after the fright of the earth tremor. But once they got going, it was really quite fun. The torches were good powerful ones and it was comforting to feel the rope around their waists.

They hadn't gone far when Kevin made a suggestion: 'Shouldn't we be marking our route with something?'

Tom stopped. 'What do you mean, Kev?'

'You know how in films and books people always leave a trail, so they can find their way back if they need to. We could do the same, er, just in case . . .' He didn't want to frighten Anna by adding in case they couldn't get out the other end.

'Good idea!' Tom praised him. 'What'll we use as a marker?'

'I'll see if there's a ball of string in the rucksack,' said Kevin, swinging it off his back and crouching down to rummage through it. He fished around inside it for a moment.

'No, no string, I'm afraid. There's quite a lot of paper though.' He held up a sheaf of A4 paper held together with a giant paper clip. 'We could leave a paper trail.'

'Let's have a look,' said Tom, taking the bundle. He looked at the sheets. They were covered in Alan's small, neat handwriting. Tom could pick out words like '*stratum*', '*troglodyte caves*' and '*hypothesis*'. 'Uh oh,' he shook his head. 'This is all Alan's sciencey stuff. We'd better not tear it up. We need something else.'

Kevin stuffed the paper back into the rucksack. Then he had a brainwave.

'I know,' he shouted, causing a booming echo that made them all laugh. 'We'll use my shorts! I hate this pair with stupid Bugs Bunny on them. My granny sent them to me. They're so uncool. I'll rip bits off and shove them in between the rocks to make a trail.'

Tom and Anna giggled as Kevin pulled the hated shorts down and started to rip strips off them. He grinned happily as he did it. 'I'll leave a bit every twenty paces,' he announced.

The children continued on their way. Suddenly the passage became a huge chamber. Tom swung the torch around. 'Look, stalagmites!' he called.

'Mega!' gasped Kevin. And they were. There were hundreds of tall spikes stretching up towards the roof of the chamber. Above their heads, an equal number of stone stalactites were reaching down to meet them.

'In another zillion years or so they'll join up and make columns,' Tom explained to Anna.

Anna stared wide-eyed.

They reluctantly left the cavern and carried on through the cave. Tom kept flicking the torch beam up to check that the orange layer of rock was still there. Kevin counted his paces and after every twenty he stuffed another piece of his shorts into a suitable spot.

Then the passage split into two. A large tunnel branched off to the left, a smaller one to the right.

'Which way?' asked Kevin. 'Left, I hope.'

'Nope!' said Tom, checking for the orange stratum. 'The rock goes this way and so must we.'

'Shame,' sighed Kevin. He'd have preferred the easier route.

It was a bit of a squeeze in places and at one point they had to splash through an underwater stream. But they went on undaunted. Anna didn't say a word. She clung trustingly to Tom's hand. 'She's a good kid,' thought Tom.

Then they came to another fork.

'Where's the orange?' asked Kevin. 'Ah, there it is.' He picked up a flash of orange with his torch in one passageway.

'No, Kev, the orange stuff is here,' Tom contradicted him, shining his torch into the other passageway.

'But it's orange here,' Kevin insisted. 'Look!' He shone his torch into the passageway again. There was orange all right, but now that he looked closer he could see that it wasn't a layer of rock. In fact it was a round patch of orange, sort of animal shaped. It seemed to have legs too. He was very puzzled.

Tom came over and peered over Kevin's shoulder. For a moment or two he couldn't make out what it was, and then he realised.

'Kev, Kev!' he cried in excitement. 'It's a cave painting.'

'Hey, cool!' cried Kevin. 'I've discovered a cave painting. Good for me!'

'And you know what it means?' Tom went on.

'That I'll be mega rich and famous?' Kevin suggested hopefully.

'No, well, maybe. But it means we are probably near, or even in, the troglodyte caves. That cave painting was done by the troglodytes. We must be nearly through!'

Kevin whooped with joy. The echo pinged around their eyes and made them all laugh. They all started making silly noises.

'Whoopeee-eee! Yoo-hoo! Aieee!'

It felt so good! Their amazing adventure was nearly over.

16 A Happy Reunion

Alan and Mum hiked as fast as they could along the hillside path and eventually they reached the troglodyte caves. They looked up at the mass of cave entrances above them.

'Which one will the children come out of?' asked Mum, struggling for breath.

Alan cleared his throat. 'I'm not exactly sure. That's what I had planned to find out tomorrow in my exploration. The orange stratum I told you about is found in all the top caves.' He pointed to a row of cave entrances about twenty metres above them. 'It'll definitely be one of those.'

'Find them, Alan,' pleaded Mum. She knew she couldn't possibly climb up the cliff-face. The long hard hike had left her body racked with pain.

Alan helped her into one of the lower caves so she could rest. Then he began scrambling up the craggy slope to the top caves. He was feeling quite tired now and the niggling doubt at the back of his mind was beginning to grow. What if he was completely wrong? What if the cave systems didn't join up? What if he didn't find the children?

He shook his head. It was too late to think like

that. All he could do now was hope and pray that he hadn't made a ghastly mistake.

He crawled the last few metres to the upper caves. He pulled himself into the first entrance and crept into the cave until it grew too dark to see. 'I wish I'd thought to keep a torch for myself,' he mused. He stopped still and listened, but all he could hear was a faint dripping of water.

'Hallo-o!' he called into the dark. His echo called back to him: 'Hallo-o!' Then nothing.

He moved on to the next cave and did the same thing. Again nothing. Then he went into the third cave. This time he crept in a bit further, using his sense of touch to take him deeper into the cave. He paused and drew a breath ready to shout again. And that's when he heard it – faint but distinct: 'Barrrbeee!'

Suddenly weak with relief, Alan leaned his head against the side of the cave. He could hear the children! He had been right about the caves! He shouted back at once: 'Cooeee! It's Alan!'

Deep in the cave, the three children had run out of silly noises to make and had started to shout out names of TV characters or toys. They had been through most of the cartoons on the Children's Channel and were working their way through their toy cupboards.

It was Anna, of course, who had shouted 'Barrrbeee' first, and then the boys had joined in. Kevin was about to bellow 'Action Man' when he heard a muffled sound.

'What was that?' asked Kevin. 'It wasn't us.'

'Shh, listen,' hissed Tom. Could it be Alan and Mum? He hardly dared hope so.

'Maybe it's a cave bear,' teased Kevin.

'Shut up!' said Tom, digging his elbow into Kevin's ribs sharply.

The three children listened again, more intently this time. But Alan was listening too so there was complete silence in the cave.

Alan called again, and so did Tom at the exact same moment.

'It's Alan.' 'We're here.'

The two echoes rumbled round the cave walls together.

'It's him, I'm sure. It's Alan,' squealed Kevin, deciphering the tangle of sound. 'Come on, let's get out of here.'

The children charged along as fast as they could. Meanwhile, Alan eased himself a little further into the passage.

'This way! I'm here!' he called into the darkness. He heard answering calls and suddenly caught a glimpse of light as Tom's torch shone towards him.

'I'm here!' he called one last time, as Tom's torch picked out his face.

'Alan! We're safe at last!' Tom cheered.

Anna dashed forward, madly scrabbling over the rocky floor to get to Alan. The two boys dived after her. Suddenly they found themselves in Alan's arms.

'Thank heavens you're OK!' muttered Alan fervently, hugging them all. 'Come on, someone's waiting to see you!'

'You saved Mum?' cried Tom.

'I sure did!' said Alan smiling.

'Thanks 'lan!' shrieked a happy Anna.

'You saved us too!' added Kevin. 'Your caves are brill. Hey, you'll never guess what we found.'

Kevin chattered away about the cave painting while Alan untied the rope tying them together.

'Really?' Alan was fascinated. 'Wow, that's quite a discovery, Kevin. You'll have to show me sometime.'

'No problem!' grinned Kevin. 'Bugs bunny will show us the way!'

Anna giggled, but poor Alan looked baffled.

'Kev left a trail of bits of his Bugs Bunny shorts, you see,' explained Tom.

Alan nodded wisely.

As soon as they reached the cave entrance, they started crawling down the cliff-face to where

Mum was resting. She dragged herself out of her shelter and waved to them as best she could, tears of joy rolling down her cheeks.

'Be careful, everyone!' she called up to them.

It was a happy moment when Alan and the children finished slithering down the cliff-face and they were all reunited with Mum. The two boys jabbered away in a frenzy about everything that had happened. Anna was content just to curl up in Mum's lap.

When the excitement died down, Alan hustled them all back into Mum's shelter.

'We'll wait here for help,' he pointed out. 'There's not much more we can do for now, we're all exhausted. And I don't want us to split up any more. My nerves can't stand it!'

'Will help come?' asked Kevin anxiously.

'Yes, in time,' said Alan. 'Remember when I said I'd looked for you in the emergency shelters? Well, there had been some seismic activity very early yesterday morning – earth tremors. This activity was recorded at a nearby research station. The scientists there alerted the authorities to the fact that some volcanic activity was imminent. The authorities then organised an evacuation of this whole area. TV announcements were made, leaflets were sent out to all the houses, that kind of thing.'

'That's what that yellow soggy thing was then,' exclaimed Tom.

Alan looked confused and so Mum explained.

'We went off to Futuroscope very early yesterday morning and we got home very late. It was raining heavily and when we found the soggy yellow piece of paper on the doorstep we couldn't read it and so we threw it out. It must have been one of those official warnings.'

'Yes, it was,' said Alan. 'Anyway, they set up a number of emergency shelters for the evacuees. I trailed round all of them trying to find you. Then, as you were tourists, I figured you might have missed the warnings. So when all hell broke loose this morning, I went out to look for you.'

'Thank goodness you did!' smiled Mum, taking Alan's hand in hers.

'So, the situation is under control. There are bound to be some search parties coming out of the village now that conditions have improved,' Alan finished.

Tom went to the cave entrance and looked out. A huge cloud still hung over the Puy de Canard, but there was less ash and dust falling and no new lava was flowing.

'Has it finished erupting?' he asked Alan.

'I doubt it,' said Alan. 'Most eruptions go on

for around ten days. Some go on a lot longer. But I'd say the worst is over for now.'

Tom sat down again and leaned against the rocky wall, content to wait for as long as it took. He was exhausted, but happy too – happy that they were all safe. Kevin crawled over next to him.

'Wow, what an adventure. What'll my Mum and Dad say?'

'They'll probably say you are never, ever to go on holiday with that dreadful Donoghue boy again!' grinned Tom.

'Who cares!' chuckled Kevin. 'What an adventure it was!'

Tom looked across at Mum, Anna and Alan. Anna was asleep in Mum's lap. Mum was leaning against Alan, talking to him quietly, still holding his hand. Alan had his other arm around Mum's shoulder. Tom realised he'd be seeing a lot more of Alan. Then he thought about how the gîte and the car were almost certainly destroyed by lava, and how they had nothing left except what they were wearing. And in Kevin's case, that wasn't much!

'Actually, Kev,' he said, turning to his friend. 'I think the adventure is only just beginning . . .'

The End

Watch out for other books from

Stephanie Dagg